Magical Mix-Ups

Pets
and
Parties

First U.S. edition 2013

ISBN 978-0-7636-6371-1

13 14 15 16 17 18 BVG 10 9 8 7 6 5 4 3 2 1

Printed in Berryville, VA, U.S.A.

This book was typeset in Bell MT.
The illustrations were created digitally.

Nosy Crow
an imprint of
Candlewick Press
99 Dover Street
Somerville, Massachusetts 02144

www.nosycrow.com
www.candlewick.com

Magical Mix-Ups

Pets and Parties

Marnie Edwards * Leigh Hodgkinson

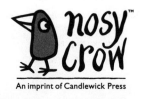

nosy crow™

An imprint of Candlewick Press

Who's Who in MIXTOPIA

Emerald the Witch

Boris

Princess Sapphire

Emerald's toad

Sapphire's dad, the King

Sapphire's mom, the Queen

who's who at the
TIP-TOP
THEATER

Agatha, the Ringmaster

Dinky, the Amazing
Juggling Cat

Toffee, Tilly,
and Tumble

Fluffy the
Rabbit

Darren

the Acrobatic Guinea Pigs

the Dancing Dog

You'll need these. . . .

Drawing
TOOLS

Using different tools helps
create great drawings.

PENCIL

COLORED PENCIL

CRAYON

Decorating TOOLS

Use these to add extra SPARKLE and MAGIC.

Sequins

Candy wrappers

Tinfoil

Glitter

Drawing Tips

Turn to the back of the book for drawing and design ideas!

glitter
at the
READY
- - - - -

GET
SET
- - -

GO!

Chapter 1

The PERFECT Pet

Mixtopia is a magical land where all sorts of amazing things happen. It's home to a lovely princess named Sapphire, who lives in the castle, and a scruffy little witch named Emerald, who lives in the cottage next door. They are the best of friends!

Draw more Mixtopian birds.

Design a "Welcome to Mixtopia" sign.

Lots more colorful flowers, please.

Draw more candy
in the sky.

Add some patterns
to the turrets.

Add
more castle
windows.

One day, Sapphire is sitting on Emerald's comfy old sofa, watching Emerald play a game of Spiders and Ladders with her trusty toad, Boris. She sighs wistfully.
"I wish I had a pet," she says.

Design a pattern on the sofa.

"Could you have one for your birthday?" says Emerald.
"Mom won't let me," replies her friend glumly.
"She said I'd play with it for five minutes, and
then guess who'd be left looking after it?"
"Who?" asks Emerald.
"I have no idea!" Sapphire sighs again, and
Emerald pats her sympathetically
on the shoulder.

Great-
Uncle Twinkletoes?

Boris?

Tula, the fairy
who lives in the garden?

Who
would end up
looking after
Sapphire's pet?

Emerald and Boris get some snacks
while Sapphire daydreams about owning a pet.
A **hamster** would be nice,

or a *goldfish*...

or a

Pony!

Draw curly ribbons in the pony's mane.

Add a big curly groomed tail.

Sapphire imagines riding on the back of a beautiful little pony, with the ribbons braided into its mane matching the ones in her hair. "I would look after a pet—I would!" she mutters fiercely, making Boris jump and drop his spider cookies all over the floor.

SPLAT!

Draw spider cookies all over the floor.

Sapphire shows Emerald her scrapbook, where she's been sticking pictures of her favorite animals. She's given them all excellent names!

SAPPHIRE'S

Miss Honeywoofle

Color Sapphire's nails.

Add names to the animals.

Add pictures and drawings to fill the scrapbook.

FAVORITE animals

cratcher

Captain CReakyclaws

Put a picture of your favorite animal here.

Sapphire's birthday is in two days. Maybe her mom will change her mind by then. . . .

october

1	2	3	4	5	
7	8	9 MY BIRTHDAY!	10	What other fun stuff is Sapphire up to?	
13	14	15	16 (boo, hiss)→	17 tidy up Royal Toy Cupboard	
19	20 broomstick flying lesson with Em	21	22	23	24 tiara shopping
25 Decorate the calendar with doodles.	27	28	29	30	
31	1	2	3	4	5

Chapter 2

PeRfect
PRESeNtS?

Draw family portraits in the frames.

Draw hands on the clock face to show the right time.

Design an ornate picture frame here.

Sapphire's birthday finally arrives. Beside herself with excitement, she rushes down the castle stairs just as the clock strikes six.

Decorate the
Royal Stairs.

The Royal Breakfast Table has been set for a birthday breakfast, and next to her place is a pile of beautifully wrapped presents. They're all shapes and sizes, and they look amazing!

Draw another stack of cards for Sapphire here.

Sapphire

Design the wrapping paper on this present.

1. What's in this package?
_____ fizh Suffanimal

2. And this one?
_____ chocelet _____

3. How about this one?
_____ piggy bank _____

Sapphire

Add a big pile of towering presents here.

Sapphire's parents enter the room, yawning. "I thought I heard you galloping down the stairs, darling," says the Queen. "Could you try to be a little more ladylike?" "Or stay in bed a bit longer?" mutters the King.

What kind of juice is this?

What do the King and Queen eat for breakfast?

Fill up the glasses.

But Sapphire is busy studying her presents. That one looks rabbit-shaped. And did that one just move? Oh, how she hopes one is a pet!

Ten minutes later, Sapphire is eating her breakfast a little sadly, surrounded by wrapping paper and ribbon. A beautiful tiara glitters next to her glass of orange juice, and she's really looking forward to wearing the sparkly dress to her party later on.

What is in this box?

Decorate Sapphire's birthday cards.

Fill her breakfast bowl with milk and cereal.

But none of her lovely new things can cuddle up with her.

After breakfast, Sapphire goes over to see Emerald.
Her friend throws open the door and gives her an
enormous hug. "Happy birthday, Sapphire!" she cries
while Boris hops around, blowing a party horn.
"I hope you like your present!"
says Emerald. "I know it's not a pet,
but we think it's the next best thing!
Now, where did I put it?"

Add lots of
big colorful
balloons.

Draw a tooting
party horn here.

Draw an
exploding party
popper.

Boris points at her hat, where
an envelope has been tucked for
safekeeping. "Ah, yes!" she cries,
and hands it to Sapphire.

"Ooh, thank you!" cries her friend, ripping it open in excitement and pulling out three sparkly tickets.

FOR ONE MAGICAL DAY ONLY!

Agatha
and her
AMAZING ANIMALS

appearing at the Tip-Top Theater
curtain up at midday

you won't believe your eyes!

Add sparkles to the tickets.

What has Emerald written on Sapphire's birthday card?

dear Sapphire

Draw a picture of Agatha here.

What animals might be in the show?

Sapphire is so excited, she can't speak!
"Let's go!" cries Emerald, whistling
for her broom. "We don't want to be late!"

Draw Sapphire's excited face.

Draw a surprised bird flying past.

Add ribbons and streamers to Emerald's broom.

Add clouds and a rainbow to create a magical sky.

Chapter 3

CURTAIN

UP

After a thrilling ride that plays havoc with Sapphire's hair, the three friends arrive at the TIP-TOP THEATER.

BROOM ROOM

Design the Tip-Top Theater sign.

Add more brooms in the broom room.

While Emerald checks her broom into the broom room, Sapphire and Boris buy armfuls of treats and a program. On the front is a picture of a sleek black-and-white cat. "Dinky, the Amazing Juggling Cat!" reads Sapphire excitedly.

Draw Sapphire's windswept hair.

TIP TOP TREATS

Who is selling the treats?

What yummy treats are for sale?

Sherbet Stars

Draw Dinky on the program here.

FIZZY MOONS

They go through the doors into the auditorium and look around in wonder. The theater is beautiful, with swirly wallpaper, a gold ceiling, and red velvet seats. These are filled with people chattering excitedly and laughing.

Decorate the ceiling with gold candy wrappers.

Finish the pattern on the curtains.

Fill the seats with people.

Add swirly wallpaper.

Everyone is really looking forward to the show!

Emerald and Sapphire take their seats in the Royal Box. "Oh, look!" cries Sapphire, pointing at the extra chair, where a large black-and-white cat is curled up. The cat purrs sleepily as Sapphire tickles her behind the ears. "She looks like Dinky, the Amazing Juggling Cat," she whispers to Emerald. "What's she doing here?"

What animals might be appearing in the show?

Decorate the front of the Royal Box.

Can you finish the pattern
on the curtains?

Add more
decorations to
Agatha's cloak.

ZAP

ZAP!

More magic sound effects, please!

The lights go down, and Sapphire is delighted when the cat climbs onto her lap and falls asleep. A spotlight appears at the front of the stage, and a tall, elegant figure steps into the light. It's Agatha! "Welcome, everyone!" she cries. "I'm sorry to say that Dinky, the Amazing Juggling Cat, will not be appearing today after all." The audience groans.

"But the show must go on!" cries Agatha. The audience cheers. "Prepare to be amazed!"

The curtains swish open, and the music starts.
Three guinea pigs come running and tumbling
onto the stage, then climb up onto a trapeze.
Soon they are flying through the air and
somersaulting all over the place.
They are Toffee, Tilly, and Tumble,
Animal Acrobats Extraordinaire!

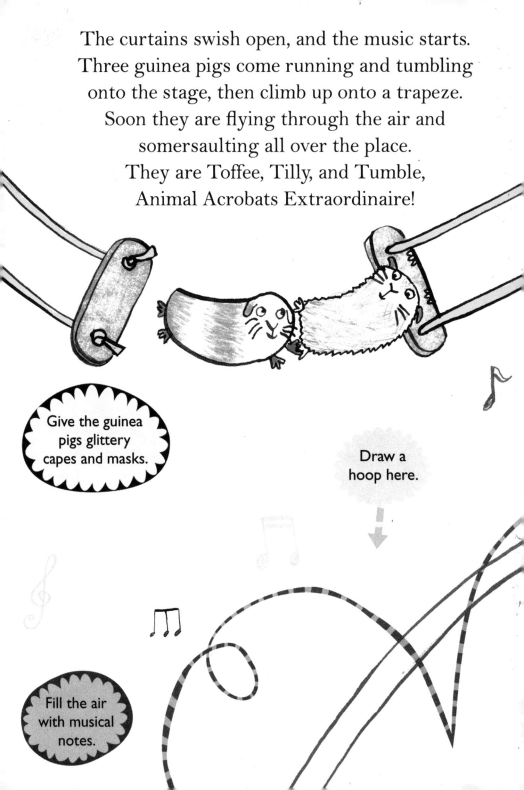

Give the guinea
pigs glittery
capes and masks.

Draw a
hoop here.

Fill the air
with musical
notes.

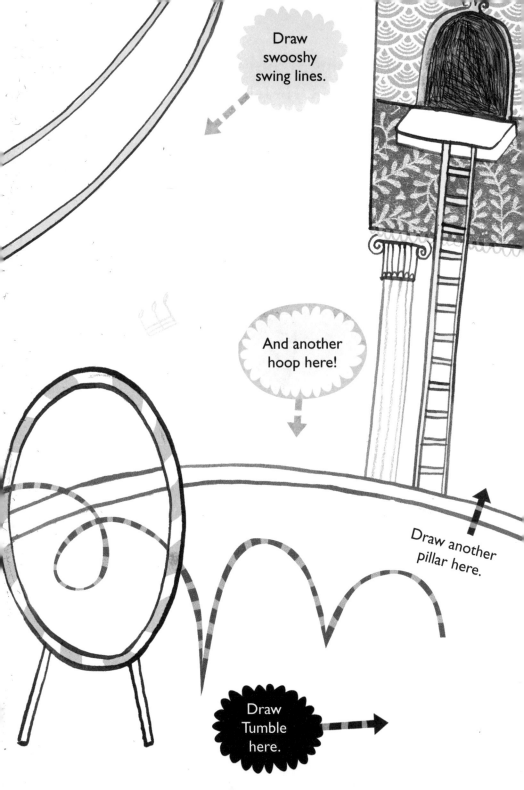

The audience claps as the guinea pigs bow. Next up is Fluffy the Rabbit. He takes off his top hat and pulls a never-ending string of colorful handkerchiefs out of it. Sapphire hugs Dinky in excitement, and the cat opens one eye, then goes back to sleep.

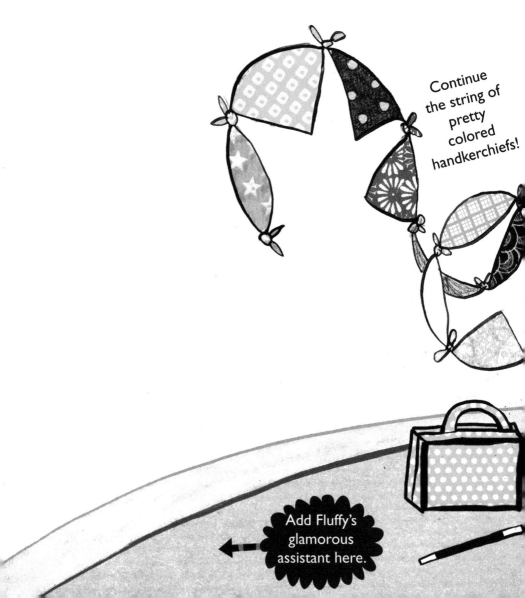

Continue the string of pretty colored handkerchiefs!

Add Fluffy's glamorous assistant here.

Darren the Dancing Dog takes the stage next. He twirls and leaps across the stage and even stands on his head! The audience has never seen anything like it, and they think he is the best dancing dog in the whole world!

After lots more fabulous acts, everyone comes back on stage to take a bow. Then Agatha steps up to the front.

Draw the final incredible act here!

A drum rolls, then she pulls out her magic wand and cries, "Abracadabra!"

A loud BANG is heard and Agatha and her amazing animals disappear in a puff of smoke. What a fantastic ending to a fantastic show!

Add more scribbly smoke puffs.

Add more sound effects

Chapter 4

A new ARRIVAL

It's time to go home. "Bye, kitty," says Sapphire, giving the cat a final cuddle. When they get to the theater door, they bump into a worried-looking Agatha. "You haven't seen my cat, Dinky, have you?" she asks. "She's supposed to be sleeping, but I can't find her anywhere!"

Draw another taxi here.

Who is on board this bus?

Decorate the bus.

The girls quickly take Agatha back to the Royal Box, but it's empty! "Don't worry, Agatha," says Sapphire. "We'll help you look for her." Agatha points to a candy wrapper on the floor. "Dinky loves candy— maybe she's left a trail."

Add more bits of candy wrappers to the trail.

They follow the trail of wrappers backstage to where all the costumes are kept. A closet door is open, and mewing sounds are coming from inside. . . .

Scatter fancy shoes on the floor.

Draw a pattern on Sapphire's dress.

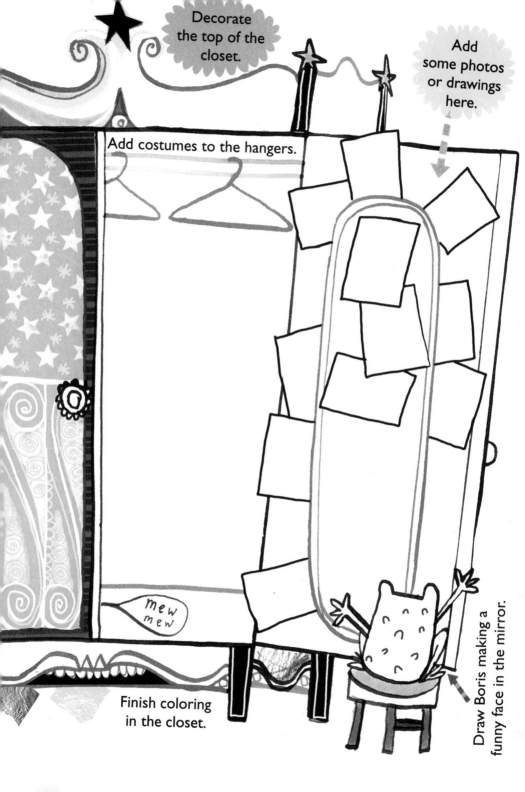

Decorate the top of the closet.

Add some photos or drawings here.

Add costumes to the hangers.

mew mew

Finish coloring in the closet.

Draw Boris making a funny face in the mirror.

Draw lots more love hearts.

Sapphire opens the door gently and gasps in surprise. There, snuggled up on a pair of frilly bloomers, is Dinky and a tiny white kitten! "Oh!" cries Sapphire, falling in love.

Agatha gathers up Dinky while Sapphire gently lifts the little kitten into her arms. They go outside to Agatha's van, where her animals are waiting. "Why don't you all come to my birthday party!" cries Sapphire.

Color in Agatha's hair and mask.

Color in Emerald's skirt.

What is the license-plate number on Agatha's van?

Pile Toffee, Tilly, and Tumble's little suitcases up here.

Add Darren's suitcases, too.

Draw Dinky looking out the window.

Is Boris in here?

Agatha & her Amazing Animals

Decorate the van with flowers and stickers.

It's agreed! Everyone heads off to the castle.
Sapphire travels in Agatha's van, cuddling
the white kitten all the way home.

Chapter 5

PARTY TIme!

As Emerald flies over the castle, she can see that it has been beautifully decorated for Sapphire's party. Flags are flying, and the lawns are set up for fun and games!

What does this banner say?

Add a bell to the bell tower.

Draw funny faces on the bouncy hopping balls.

What other games are set up on the lawn?

Agatha's van pulls up, too, and all the animals scamper out. Everyone laughs as Tilly, Tumble, and Toffee ride around on a bicycle. . . .

Draw big smiles on everyone's faces.

Draw Tilly on top, busily whirling Boris around!

Now add Tumble balancing on Tilly's head, too.

Add more wobble lines to the bicycle.

Give the horn a big HONK sound!

especially when they grab Boris and whirl him around with them, too!

"Quick, Boris!" she says. "We need to get changed."
She rummages in her closet while Boris puts on his
best bow tie.

Sapphire is getting ready, too. She tries on her new dress, which fits beautifully, and puts on her new tiara.

Add color to Sapphire's many bottles of nail polish.

Draw the pile of shoes Sapphire decided NOT to wear!

Design a pattern on the rug.

Meanwhile, carriages are rolling up outside, dropping off all of Sapphire's party guests!

Add another fancy carriage here.

These princes and princesses all need crowns!

Fluffy the Rabbit pulls a huge present out of his top hat and adds it to the enormous pile by the fountain.

Draw a big colorful bow around the present.

Decorate the wrapping paper.

Darren the Dancing Dog pirouettes perfectly over to the refreshments table and helps himself to a sausage.

Add big curly straws to the glasses.

Add starry ice cubes to the pitcher.

Fill the plate with tasty sausages.

The sun is shining, and the band strikes up a merry tune. Sapphire's birthday party has begun!

Chapter 6

The BEST present of ALL

WIBBLE

Color in Sapphire's skirt.

Soon, a hilarious game of freeze tag is under way.

Draw more guests in funny positions.

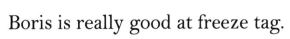

Boris is really good at freeze tag.

Finish drawing the Royal Cupcakes.

Add more chocolate rolls to the pile.

Make more ice-cream sundaes.

Add some more sandwiches.

Sapphire's mom calls everyone inside. The table is piled high with sandwiches, cupcakes, and drinks. And amazing sundaes in every flavor!

Sapphire makes sure the kitten
has plenty to eat and drink, too.

Then the lights go out and a fabulous birthday cake is brought in. Everyone sings "Happy Birthday" to Sapphire.

When everyone has had cake, Agatha finds Sapphire and Emerald. "I must go, darlings," she says. "We've had such a lovely time, but my animals need their beauty sleep!" Sapphire gives the white kitten a hug and holds him out to Agatha. Her eyes fill with tears, but she sniffs bravely.

Agatha looks at her. "I think you should talk to your mom again. . . ."

Draw a little tear falling from Sapphire's eye.

What sort of slippers does Fluffy wear?

Soon Sapphire comes flying back across the lawn from the castle. "Mom says I can keep him because it's my birthday!" Agatha is so pleased that she magically turns the castle gardens into a snowy wonderland.
"I'll call him Snowy!"

Draw a jolly snowman here.

Decorate the curtains.

Draw Sapphire's bedside lamp here.

What bedtime book is Sapphire going to read?

After a wonderful day, Emerald and Boris and all the guests head home. Sapphire puts on her pajamas and climbs into bed.

Draw her new tiara hanging on her tiara tree.

Draw Sapphire's party dress hanging up.

The small white kitten curled up on her pillow gives a tiny sneeze, and sparks fly from his whiskers.

Perhaps her kitten is magical like his mother! She gives him a hug and falls asleep, dreaming of all the fun they are going to have together.

What is Sapphire dreaming about?

The Big Picture
Draw your favorite moments from the book, and add some decorative tidbits.

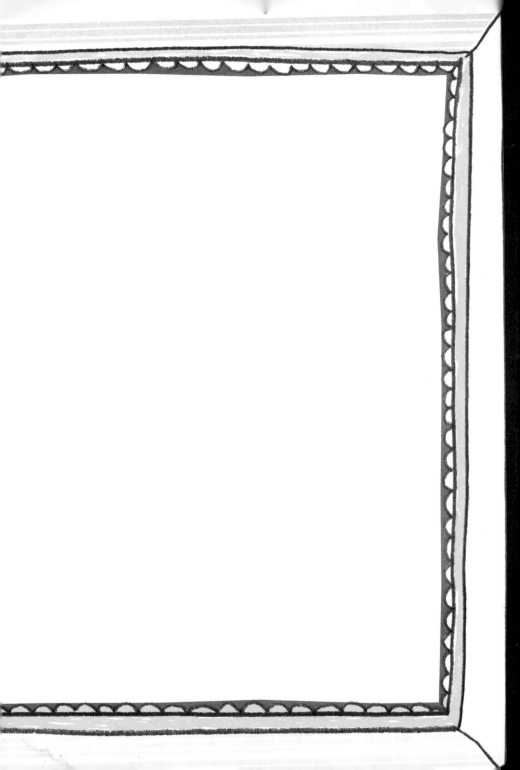

picture GLOSSARY

If you need a helping hand thinking of things to draw, then check these ideas out!

instruments

POP

POPPITY

POP

party popper

medals

FIRST
1

suitcases

TAXI

taxi

bow ties

birthday cake

Mixtopian birds

bouncy castle